The Snowman Band of Snowboggle Bend

By Cheryl Hawkinson

Illustrated by Mike Esberg

♔ Hallmark
GIFT BOOKS

The Snowman Band of Snowboggle Bend
Copyright © 2010 Hallmark Licensing, Inc.

Published by Hallmark Books,
a division of Hallmark Cards, Inc.,
Kansas City, MO 64141
Visit us on the Web at www.Hallmark.com.

Editor: Emily Osborn
Art Director: Kevin Swanson
Designer: Scott Swanson
Production Designer: Bryan Ring

ISBN: 978-1-59530-292-2

1LPR7505

Printed and bound in China
JUL10

Welcome to SNOWBOGGLE BEND

To: Emma

From: Cindy + Ken

Christmas 2010

In the far northern village
of Snowboggle Bend,
it snowed…and it snowed…
and it snowed without end.

Snow floated and fluttered
and silenced the land,
except for the sound
of the town's only band.

From a broken-down school bus
their music came soaring,
awakening animals
who'd rather be snoring.

They called themselves Snow Pack,
these talented four,
and they practiced and practiced
and practiced some more.

Snow-Joe blew sweetly
on his alto sax,
while Snow-Freddy's fingers
flew over his axe.

Snow-Tom on trumpet
could make a horn sing,
and Snow-Ken on keys
was a beautiful thing.

There was just one small problem.

No one knew they existed.

It was hard to get gigs,

but Snow Pack persisted.

Each year they made tracks

to a nearby big city

to audition for Slush Fest.

The results were not pretty.

Each year they received

a "Sorry, but no!"

from the concert's promoter,

Sir Farley Fitz Snow.

"We've got to do something,"

said Snow-Ken at last.

"Let's just GO to the Slush Fest.

It might be a blast!"

“But how do we get there?”
said Snow-Joe with a frown.
“The Snow Dome Pavilion
is way out of town.”

"Well, our bus is no help,"
sadly answered Snow-Freddy,
"Its get-up is gone
and it's hardly road-ready."

"There's someone," said Snow-Tom,
"who might fix it for us,
She's quite the mechanic,
my sister, Snow-Doris."

"I'll fix it," Sis said,
soon after arriving.
"But when I'm all finished,
then I'll do the driving."

So Snow Pack left town
with some rattling and creaking,
but at the first curve
they heard shouting and shrieking.

A huge crowd had gathered
by the Mountain Pass Ranch.
The band cried out loudly,
"Oh, no! Avalanche!"

"No one can move!
Everyone's stuck!
Goodbye, good old Slush Fest.
Man, what bad luck!"

"But where are the mammoths?"
demanded Snow-Joe.
"Our town's team of woolies
should shovel this snow!"

Sure enough, the two mammoths
showed up at the scene,
but they wouldn't budge—
they were moody and mean.

"Hey," said Snow Freddy,
"No one's leaving here soon.
We've got an audience—
let's play 'em some tunes."

So they turned up their amps
and they really got swinging.
And soon EVERYBODY
was clapping and singing.

Then someone said "Look,
the mammoths are movin'!
Who knew they liked music?
They really are groovin'!

Sure enough, the two woolies
were smiling and dancing.
You would think they were reindeer,
the way they were prancing.

Then quick as a flash
the two creatures had cleared
a path through the mountains
and everyone cheered!

When who should appear
but Sir Farley Fitz Snow,
saying, "Good job, you guys.
What a band! What a show!

"This is kind of last-minute,
but what do you say?
Could you be the star act
at the Slush Fest today?"

They all looked at each other,

then replied with a grin,

"Well, we are kind of busy,

but we'll fit you in."

If this book got you moving, grooving,
or boogying down with your bad self,
we would love to hear from you.

PLEASE SEND YOUR COMMENTS TO:
Hallmark Book Feedback
P.O. Box 419034
Mail Drop 215
Kansas City, Missouri 64141

OR E-MAIL US AT:
booknotes@hallmark.com